RUBY'S FIERY MISHAP

The Gemstone Dragons series

Opal's Time to Shine

Ruby's Fiery Mishap

RUBY'S FIERY MISHAP

Samantha M. Clark

ILLUSTRATED BY
Janelle Anderson

BLOOMSBURY
CHILDREN'S BOOKS
NEW YORK LONDON OXFORD NEW DELHI SYDNEY

BLOOMSBURY CHILDREN'S BOOKS
Bloomsbury Publishing Inc., part of Bloomsbury Publishing Plc
1385 Broadway, New York, NY 10018

BLOOMSBURY, BLOOMSBURY CHILDREN'S BOOKS, and the Diana logo
are trademarks of Bloomsbury Publishing Plc

First published in the United States of America in August 2022
by Bloomsbury Children's Books

Bloomsbury books may be purchased for business or promotional use. For information
on bulk purchases please contact Macmillan Corporate and Premium Sales Department at
specialmarkets@macmillan.com

Library of Congress Cataloging-in-Publication Data
Names: Clark, Samantha M., author. | Anderson, Janelle O., illustrator.
Title: Ruby's fiery mishap / by Samantha M. Clark ; illustrated by Janelle O. Anderson.
Description: New York : Bloomsbury Children's Books, [2022] |
Series: Gemstone dragons ; 2 | Audience: Grades 2–3
Summary: Ruby is the youngest Gemstone Dragon and very passionate about being the best.
But when an attempt at showing off turns into a dangerous forest fire, will Ruby be able to
master her power?—Provided by publisher.
Identifiers: LCCN 2021048233 (print) | LCCN 2021048234 (e-book)
ISBN 978-1-5476-0892-8 (paperback) • ISBN 978-1-5476-0894-2 (e-book)
Subjects: CYAC: Fantasy. | Magic—Fiction. | Dragons—Fiction. | Ability—Fiction. |
Self-control—Fiction. | LCGFT: Fantasy fiction.
Classification: LCC PZ7.1.C579 Rub 2022 (print) |
LCC PZ7.1.C579 (e-book) | DDC [Fic]—dc23
LC record available at https://lccn.loc.gov/2021048233
LC ebook record available at https://lccn.loc.gov/2021048234

Book design by Jeanette Levy
Typeset by Westchester Publishing Services
Printed in the U.S.A.
2 4 6 8 10 9 7 5 3 1

To find out more about our authors and books
visit www.bloomsbury.com and sign up for our newsletters.

For Bethany, who believes,

and for Taru, her heart

GEMSTONE DRAGONS

RUBY'S FIERY MISHAP

chapter one

TRICKY TRICKS

A hint of a storm swirled around Gemstone Valley, but no one minded because the sun was peeking through the clouds and every magical creature was in the fields watching the Gemstone Dragons do tricks with their special powers.

Unifoals, young goblins, and gnome tykes oohed and aahed as Topaz spun in the air until her light power looked like a giant pulsing star. Opal used her power of invisibility to play a game of Now You See Me, Now You Don't. Aquamarine lifted chunks of water out of the river so Pearl could power it into ice sculptures.

Everyone cheered and laughed.

Everyone was having fun.

Everyone except Ruby.

"I'll never be able to use my power right! I'm useless," Ruby cried, as another one of her fireballs sizzled out. "I'm the most useless Gemstone Dragon that's ever lived."

"Oh Ruby," said Opal, her rainbow-streaked scales shimmering as she became visible. "You're not useless at all. You're a wonderful Gemstone Dragon."

"But I never get anything right!" Ruby hung her head.

"That's not true. You do lots of things well." Opal gave Ruby a big smile, but it didn't make Ruby feel any better.

Topaz stopped spinning and landed next to them. "Wha . . . wha . . ." She was out of breath from spinning so fast in the air. "What were you trying to do?"

"Just a trick, like you and the other dragons, but my fire keeps going all over the place."

"I'm sure it's not that bad," Topaz said. "Go on. Show us."

Ruby sighed but said, "Okay."

She took a deep breath. Then the gemstone on her chest began to glow as she blew out a ball of fire. It was small and manageable, but Ruby started to imagine all the bad things that could go wrong.

What if it grew really big and she couldn't control it? What if it lit the grass on fire? What if it fell on Topaz and Opal?

As she was thinking these things, her fireball grew bigger and bigger and bigger. Topaz and Opal had been about to clap their paws at Ruby's power, but the fireball wobbled in the air. Ruby gave a little cry, scared that all the bad things she had imagined would come true. She quickly breathed all the fire back in, then shook her head.

"See? I can't make it work."

"You'll get it," Topaz said. "Don't wo—"

"You have to concentrate more, Ruby," Diamond shouted from where he was using his wind power to lift the unifoals into the air as they giggled. "Here, watch me."

Diamond scrunched up his face in concentration and breathed out a small fireball. Then the diamond in his chest began to glow as he made the wind push the flames so they twisted into the sky. The Gemstone Valley children applauded loudly.

Diamond grinned and bowed down low to his audience.

Ruby's cheeks felt hot and she glared at the ground so no one would see. Diamond had just done a trick with fire and he only had the small amount of fire breath that all the Gemstone Dragons had. Ruby had much more fire power because of her gemstone, but she couldn't control it enough to even bounce a fireball.

"Come on," Diamond said, turning back to Ruby. "Now you try. Concentrate hard."

The youngsters and the other Gemstone Dragons gathered around. Opal cheered. "You can do it, Ruby!"

"Show us a trick," shouted a unifoal called Honeydoo.

"Yes, show us something uni-mazing!" said another unifoal called Canterlope.

They pranced around until Diamond told them to hush.

Now Ruby was even more anxious. Her tummy felt as if the magma cakes she'd had for breakfast were boiling all over again.

What if she couldn't do the trick?

Topaz leaned close and squeezed Ruby's paw. "You'll be brilliant."

Ruby wasn't so sure, but now that everyone from Gemstone Valley was watching, she had to try.

"Concentrate just like I told you," Diamond said, showing her his concentration face. "That's all it takes."

Ruby stopped herself from scowling at Diamond, then scrunched up her snout, trying to act as much like she was concentrating as she could. She breathed a ball of fire onto her paw, pulled power from her gemstone, then bounced the fireball in the air.

It stayed intact! *Maybe I can use my power after all*, Ruby thought.

Now she had to do a trick. As her red scales rippled, she breathed out another fireball and another. With each one, the youngsters oohed and aahed. Ruby smiled. She liked making them happy.

She began to juggle the fireballs, sending one high into the air and the others after it.

Honeydoo, Canterlope, and the other youngsters cheered. Ruby beamed. A bloom of happiness burst inside her. She wanted to do more. Her gemstone glowed brighter as she juggled the fireballs faster.

"You're doing it, Ruby," Diamond said. "Keep concentrating."

Ruby scrunched her snout again. She *was* doing it. She was doing a trick! Maybe Diamond had been right and she did have to concentrate. If she concentrated even more, maybe she could do an even better trick! She tried to make her concentration face even stronger as she thought of what she could do with the fireballs next—before they got out of control again and did something bad.

Suddenly, one of the balls blazed bigger.

"Oh no!" Ruby panicked, worrying that she'd lost her concentration.

Then another ball flared. Then the third. Each fireball swelled up, sparks spitting from them. Ruby couldn't stop them!

She tried to breathe the fire back in, but only two fireballs obeyed. The third crashed onto the ground.

FWOOF!

The grass around the dragons lit up with small flames, and Opal and Topaz screeched.

"Push dirt over it," said Amber, running up to help them as her light orange scales shimmered.

Opal, Amber, and Topaz dug their claws into the soil, then kicked dirt over the grass until every bit of fire was extinguished.

Ruby flopped onto the ground. "See! I'll never get it right." The bloom of happiness withered inside her.

"You have to concentrate harder. Try it more next time," Diamond said, giving Ruby an encouraging smile.

But she didn't feel like concentrating, and she didn't feel very encouraged.

"Have patience," Opal said. "You're still young. It'll come."

"Just relax," Topaz said.

"No, concentrating is better," Diamond said. "And eating more nitrogen."

"Try standing with a strong foundation like I do," Amber said. "And practice. Lots of practice."

"Don't forget to drink lots of water! That

always makes my power work really well,"
Aquamarine said, grinning.

Ruby looked from one dragon to another,
her mind spinning with all their advice.
"It doesn't matter what I do," she wailed.
"I'll never get my power right. Never!"

Then she stormed off, hoping more than
anything that she was wrong.

chapter two

A SNOWY PROBLEM

Ruby flew over to the clearing next to the Friendly Forest. She wanted to be alone. She appreciated all the dragons' advice, but how could she know who was right? It seemed like nothing she tried made it any easier for her to control her fire power.

One piece of advice did stick out to her, though. Amber had said she should practice, and that gave Ruby an idea.

"I'll build another bonfire," she mumbled to herself.

Opal had once helped Ruby make a little bonfire in the field outside her bedcave so she could practice without getting a sore throat from making so much fire. With the bonfire, Ruby found it much easier to control the flames. To get really good at her power, she could practice with a bonfire again.

"But the fire kept going out on the little one I had before," she said. "This time I'll build a giant bonfire! Then I can practice as long as I need to become as good as all the other Gemstone Dragons."

Ruby spent the next few hours gathering sticks and twigs from the floor of the Friendly Forest. She piled them up on the edge of the Crystal River into one large bonfire. With her red wings flapping, she balanced the last twig on top of the stack, then flew back to the ground and admired her work. Yes, it would do nicely.

The pile of sticks rose up in front of her like a rickety wooden tower. To Ruby, it was a tower of hope—hope that she could finally master her fire power.

The sky had turned gray as clouds high up blocked out the sun. Ruby ignored them, though. She was determined to get some tricks working today.

She took a deep breath. Then the ruby gemstone in her chest glowed red as she tapped into its power. She blew giant fireballs onto the bonfire, and the flames shot up, reaching into the sky.

"Yes!" she shouted. "Now I just have to keep practicing until I can control my fire and do perfect tricks."

Concentrating the way Diamond had told her to, Ruby pulled some of the flames from the bonfire. No one was watching her or close enough to get hurt if anything went wrong, which made everything less scary.

"If the fire gets out of control, I can just put it back on the bonfire so everything's safe," she told herself.

Her red scales rippled as she guided the flames into a glowing ball on her paw. Holding her breath, she waited for the ball to grow out of control, but it didn't. She bounced the ball on the ground, lifting it quickly so it didn't scorch the grass. It bounced! She threw it into the air, and it came right back down to her paw.

She was doing it!

Ruby balanced the ball on her paw, then flicked one side to make it spin. Round and round it went. It wobbled, but she balanced it again.

"It's working!" she shouted.

She gathered more flames from the bonfire, then pulled her giant fireball into a wide fiery hoop. With her gemstone glowing, she twisted the hoop over her head and made it dance around her belly.

"YAY!" she screamed. She was finally controlling her fire!

She pulled the ring back up and spun it on her paw. It looked beautiful, the flames flickering as they went around and around.

Until . . . *SPLOSH!*

The fire ring went up in smoke. Her paw was covered in a glob of snow.

"No!" Ruby looked at the clouds overhead. Snow had begun to fall. It was still light, and Ruby hoped it would stop. She was just getting started!

"That was uni-rific!" Canterlope ambled up with Honeydoo and Topaz.

"Yeah, Ruby!" said Topaz. "Your fire ring was amazing. We were going to play some games in Shimmering Hall but when we saw your trick, we had to come over."

Ruby smiled. "Thanks!" But she was distracted. She gazed up at the sky again. The high gray clouds were still there, but the snowflakes had stopped falling. Good.

"Can you show us something else, Ruby?" Canterlope asked. "Something just for us?"

Honeydoo nodded, the horn on her forehead glistening.

"Hmm." Ruby thought of what she could do. Canterlope was the smallest of the unifoals, just like Ruby was the smallest Gemstone Dragon. She wanted to give him a trick he'd really love. Something that would make him feel special.

She remembered one of her favorite tricks from Aquamarine. Using his gemstone power over water, he'd write dripping names in the sky. Maybe Ruby could do that with fire.

"Okay," she said. "Here's one for you."

Canterlope and Honeydoo glanced at each other excitedly. Ruby felt a swell of pride. Now she just had to do the trick properly.

As her gemstone lit up, Ruby put on her

best concentration face the way Diamond had showed her. She collected some flames from her bonfire, then stretched them into a big *C*.

Canterlope jumped up and down. "It's a *C*! Like the start of my name!"

This next part was tricky. Ruby had to keep the *C*-shaped flames swirling in the air while she pulled more fire to make the next letter. How did Aquamarine do it?

Worry crept into Ruby's brain. What if she couldn't finish the trick? She didn't want to disappoint Canterlope and Honeydoo, and she especially wanted to show Topaz how good she was getting at controlling her power.

Scrunching up her snout to concentrate

even more, Ruby held the *C* in place, then drew more fire for the *A*. But the flames in the *C* flickered and died.

"Oh," said Honeydoo, disappointed.

"That's okay," said Canterlope. "Ruby can do more. You can, can't you, Ruby?"

"I . . ." Ruby wasn't sure. She had done so well with the hoop, but now she was having problems again. Why?

"Try again, Ruby." Topaz smiled. "You're doing great."

Ruby tried to smile back, but it felt more like a grimace. She didn't think she was doing great at all, but she didn't want anyone else to know that. "Okay," she said, her voice quavering. "Here goes."

Her ruby gemstone glowed and her red

scales rippled as Ruby started to gather flames from the bonfire again. She got the *C* in the air and breathed a sigh of relief. Next she had to do the *A*. She collected more flames and formed the first half of the letter. It was working!

Her gemstone glowed brighter and she concentrated harder. The *A* came into shape. She had *CA*. She reached out for more fire, but . . .

SPLISH!

A fat glob of snow sizzled her letters into smoke. Then . . .

SPLASH!

A flurry of snow extinguished her bonfire. And . . .

SPLOSH!

A clump of snow fell right on her head.

"No!" Ruby stomped her foot. "No. No! NO!"

Canterlope and Honeydoo stepped back. Topaz moved closer to Ruby.

"It's okay. You'll do it," she said.

"I was doing it!" Ruby shouted. "You saw! I was doing it. And this snow is messing up everything."

She glared at the snow clouds above.

"I just wanted to practice and get really good like you and all the other Gemstone Dragons." Tears welled in Ruby's eyes. "But I won't be good at all if I can't practice."

She whacked her tail hard against the ground.

"It's not snowing too hard," Topaz said, trying to be helpful. "Light your bonfire again."

Ruby frowned, but her gemstone glowed as she breathed out a rush of fire onto the tower of sticks. It erupted into flames and she grinned. Then . . .

FWUMP!

Snow drenched her bonfire again. "NO! NO! NO! I just want to practice. It's not fair!"

The snow didn't let up this time. Big round snowflakes dropped from the sky, covering Ruby's bonfire.

"It's okay, Ruby," Topaz said. "You'll have lots of time to practice. You'll get it one day."

"But I want to control my power now!" Then, with her gemstone glowing brighter than ever, Ruby breathed out enough fire to light a hundred bonfires.

But the fire didn't light the tower of twigs and sticks. Her breath was so powerful, it arced all the way to the edge of the Friendly Forest.

Flames attacked the trees, and with a *FWOOF*, they caught on fire.

chapter three

SOME VERY NEEDED HELP

"Oh no!" Ruby stared at the flames shooting up the trees of the Friendly Forest. "What have I done?"

"*AAAAHHH!*" Canterlope screamed in fear, then took off running. Honeydoo cried out and ran away too.

Ruby and Topaz stared at the fire.

"You've got to do something!" Topaz said. "Make the fire go away."

Ruby tried to breathe the fire back in, but it wouldn't leave the trees. "I can't pull it back." Her eyes grew wide.

"You have to extinguish it." Topaz pointed to the forest. "If you can make the fire, you must be able to take it away. Try again!"

Worry rolled around in Ruby's tummy. What if she couldn't stop the fire? What if it burned all of the Friendly Forest? What if she destroyed Gemstone Valley?

"Okay," Ruby said, her voice shaky. "I'll try."

The ruby in her chest glowed, but only dimly. Still, she had to do anything she could. She reached out to the flames, trying to draw them away from the trees. But

instead of coming toward her, the fire leaped to another tree. *POOF*! It lit up like the others.

"No!" Ruby turned to Topaz. "I don't know what to do."

"I don't know either." Topaz glanced between the burning trees and her friend.

Ruby looked at her extinguished bonfire, then frowned at the sky. The snow had let up again, but now Ruby wished it hadn't. "Why won't the snow come down harder now?"

"That's it!" said Topaz. "Aquamarine and Pearl will be able to drown the flames with their powers over water and ice. I'll get them."

"But they'll see what I did," said Ruby.

"They'll know I failed. I want to fix this myself."

"We don't have time, Ruby!" Topaz stared at her friend. "We have to help the forest. Keep trying, but I'm going to get Aquamarine and Pearl."

Topaz opened her shimmering brown wings and took off, flying toward Sparkle Cave.

The fire was raging stronger now. Ruby gulped, trying to swallow down all her fears. She had made this problem and she had to try to fix it. But how?

She should get closer. She should concentrate more.

But she couldn't do anything. She felt frozen in place. All she could do was stare at the flames, a pit of nerves growing bigger and bigger in her tummy.

"We'll stop the fire!" Aquamarine shouted as he flew over Ruby's head toward the forest.

"Those flames are big!" shouted Pearl, following him.

Topaz landed next to Ruby. "Don't worry, they'll fix it."

Tears prickled Ruby's eyes. She had caused the blaze but felt powerless to stop it.

Aquamarine and Pearl touched down near the burning trees and immediately went to work. Aquamarine pulled water up from the river and doused the flames on the nearest tree. Pearl gathered snow from the ground and the clouds overhead and dumped it on other trees.

Soon the whole fire was out. The Friendly Forest and Gemstone Valley were saved.

Aquamarine and Pearl high-fived. "Team Water and Ice to the rescue!" Aquamarine grinned.

"Team Ice and Water, you mean," Pearl said, and they both laughed.

Ruby wished she had Opal's power and could disappear.

chapter four

A BIG DECISION

✦ ✱ ✶ ✦ ✱ ✶ ✱ ✦

"Putting out fires makes me hungry."
Aquamarine patted his belly as he strode
up to Ruby and Topaz. "Who wants sulfur
muffins?"

Pearl grinned as she walked over. "I do!
Wow, that was some fire, Ruby. You've got
a lot of power in your gemstone."

"I'm sorry I did that." Ruby stared at the
ground. "I didn't mean to hurt anything."

"We know that," said Topaz, putting her arm around Ruby's shoulder. "It was an accident."

"Good thing you told us, though," Pearl said. "Fires like that spread fast."

"Yeah, because you know how fire was invented, don't you?" Aquamarine chuckled, and before the others could answer, he blurted out, "In a blaze of glory! Get it? Blaze? Like a wildfire blaze?"

Pearl and Topaz laughed along with Aquamarine, but Ruby didn't. She watched as Pearl and Aquamarine headed back to Mineral Mountain, then she turned to the blackened trees on the edge of the Friendly Forest. "Did I kill them?"

Topaz shook her head. "Emerald will use his gemstone power to get them growing again." She looped her arm around Ruby's. "Come on, let's go get some of those sulfur muffins."

But Ruby didn't feel like celebrating. Because she had gotten angry and lost control of her power, she'd set the Friendly Forest on fire. And she was still no closer to being able to do tricks like the other Gemstone Dragons.

"You go," she told Topaz. "I want to be by myself for a while."

"You sure?"

Ruby nodded and walked away.

As Topaz trudged back to Sparkle Cave, Ruby went in the opposite direction. She didn't feel like being with anyone. She didn't feel like she deserved to be with anyone. All the other dragons were amazing. They had fantastic powers that helped people.

All Ruby's power could do was destroy. She hated it.

Ruby thought about what her power had done as she climbed up the side of Mineral Mountain. She thought about it as she wandered through the crystal fields.

And she thought about it as she weaved through the orchards.

She couldn't get the images of the burned trees out of her mind. And worse, she couldn't forget the frightened screams of Honeydoo and Canterlope.

She felt horrible.

As Ruby finally traipsed back to Sparkle Cave, she made a decision: She would never use her gemstone power again.

chapter five

GONE MISSING

The entrance to Sparkle Cave was busier than usual when Ruby got back. Dragons, unicorns, gnomes, and fairies were crowded around. Everyone was talking at once.

Ruby skirted around the outside of the group and found Topaz.

"Where have you been?" Topaz asked.

Ruby was about to tell her, but her friend continued.

"Canterlope is missing! Everyone's been searching, but no one can find him."

"What?" Ruby's heartbeat quickened. "How long has he been gone?"

"No one knows, but . . ." Topaz's voice got quiet. "No one has seen him since the fire."

Ruby gulped. She felt like the world had just crashed on top of her head.

"But he ran home with Honeydoo," she said. "We saw that."

Hadn't she seen that?

"We saw him run off," Topaz said. "But Honeydoo ran home and she said Canterlope didn't follow. He's lost!"

Ruby gasped. She couldn't believe what she was hearing.

Suddenly there was a *SWOOSH*, and Garnet thudded to the ground, his pink scales glistening as he folded up his wings. His gemstone power was speed, and Ruby realized he must've been searching high and low for Canterlope.

"Did you see anything?" Sapphire, the oldest Gemstone Dragon, strode over to Garnet. The unicorns and gnomes gathered around too.

Garnet's shoulders slumped. "No. I looked all over Mineral Mountain and the Friendly Forest, but I didn't see any sign of him."

The unicorns started murmuring among themselves. Sapphire looked worried. *All* the Gemstone Dragons looked worried.

Sapphire peered up at the sky. Night was descending. Clouds were thick and high overhead.

"Looks like we could get more snow tonight," Sapphire said, her dark blue snout sniffing the air. She turned to the unicorns standing nearby. "But don't worry. I'm sure Canterlope is safe. He's probably sleeping in a barn. Come on, dragons. We won't stop looking until we find him."

All the Gemstone Dragons trod down to Gemstone Valley. Ruby felt excited. She could make this right! She could help them find Canterlope.

"Ruby," Sapphire said gently, as she put her paw on Ruby's shoulder. "You stay here. The night could get cold and you're still a young dragon. You too, Topaz. Both of you stay inside Sparkle Cave."

"No!" Ruby felt terrible. Canterlope had

run away because of the fire. Because of her. "I want to help."

Sapphire smiled sadly. "I know you're worried, Ruby, but we'll find Canterlope. You're a smart dragon, and if there's one thing I know about being smart, it means you know what to do. Canterlope will show up soon."

Sapphire gave a nod, then walked down Mineral Mountain, leaving Ruby and Topaz behind.

"You heard Sapphire, Ruby," Topaz said. "Canterlope will be okay."

"No, Topaz!" Ruby's eyes filled with tears. "If I hadn't started that fire, Canterlope would never have run off. Now we have no idea where he is, and it's all my fault!"

Ruby spread her wings and flew into the air.

"Ruby! Where are you going?" Topaz called after her.

Ruby wasn't sure. She just wanted to do something. Before she knew it, her wings had taken her to the edge of the Friendly Forest. She gazed up at the burned trees. They looked sad and lonely, just like Canterlope must be.

Topaz landed beside Ruby. "Come on, it's getting dark. Sapphire said we should go into Sparkle Cave. There might be a storm."

Ruby sighed. "I just wanted to see. I just wanted . . ."

Her voice trailed off. Something on the ground caught her eye.

"Topaz, look!" Ruby pointed and Topaz came over to examine the spot. "Hoofprints! This is where Canterlope and Honeydoo were."

"We know that, Ruby. They ran back to Gemstone Valley."

"No, only one set of prints goes back to the valley," said Ruby. "See?"

Topaz looked. "You're right."

"The other prints go that way, down the river. That must be where Canterlope went. Come on!" Ruby started to run, following the hoofprints.

"Ruby, wait!" shouted Topaz. "We're supposed to go back to Sparkle Cave. We have to tell Sapphire. Garnet can fly over and look for Canterlope."

"It'll take too long," Ruby said, glancing toward the valley. The sky was almost black and snowflakes had started to fall. "Besides, Garnet said he already flew over the forest, but how would he be able to see Canterlope through the tops of all the trees?"

Topaz opened her mouth but didn't reply. Instead she looked at the tops of the trees. "They are dense."

"Garnet would never be able to see the ground from the sky," Ruby said. "He might see something moving, but what if Canterlope is curled up somewhere, next to a tree? Garnet wouldn't be able to see him then."

Ruby thought of Canterlope curled up all by himself and shuddered. She wouldn't want to be all by herself, and she was sure Canterlope didn't want to be either.

Topaz gave her friend a small smile. "That's why I love you, Ruby. You see things I never do. Okay, we'll tell Sapphire and they can start searching the forest on paws."

"No!" Ruby started walking in the direction of the hoofprints. "No one will believe me. They think I'm too young to know what to do."

"But it's getting dark. And it's going to snow harder." Topaz pointed at the clouds.

Ruby turned to her friend. "That's why I have to go now, Topaz. By the time we get the other dragons, the snow will be too heavy to find Canterlope. I have to help him."

"But Sapphire said—"

"Topaz!" Ruby shook her head. "Sapphire said being smart was knowing what to do. I don't know how smart I am, but I do know that this is my fault. I have to go find Canterlope right now."

She started following the hoofprints toward the forest.

Topaz sighed, then ran after her friend. She nudged her shoulder against Ruby's. "If you're so smart, you should've known your best friend wouldn't let you go alone." She grinned.

Ruby smiled back. "I guess you're pretty smart yourself."

chapter six

SOMETHING IN THE HOLLOW

Ruby gulped as they got to the edge of the Friendly Forest. She had always loved the forest, with its tall trees peering down at her from so high up. But at night, the crooked branches of the trees seemed less welcoming and more spooky.

Topaz must've been thinking the same thing. She shivered against Ruby's arm.

"I don't see his hoofprints anymore," Topaz said.

"They must be here somewhere." Ruby peered through the tree trunks, then onto the ground. "There! See that clearing in the line of trees? He probably ran in there thinking it was safe."

"You think so?" Topaz asked.

Ruby shrugged. "That's where I would have run."

They hurried into the clearing. The thin strip of land that was bare of trees wove into the forest as though it were a river with no water. After a while, Ruby stopped.

"You can't see Gemstone Valley or the Crystal River anymore!"

"We've gone far," Topaz said.

"I know. And it makes me nervous." Ruby shook her head, but then she got an idea. "Canterlope would've been nervous too. He probably went into the trees somewhere to find a short cut to get back home." She looked around. "Do you see any broken branches or twigs?"

Topaz hurried over to a bush that had been trampled. "Like this?"

Ruby nodded. "Yes! Come on." She led the way into the forest.

The night was even darker here. Between the thick clouds and the dense tree trunks, only thin moonlight was able to get through.

Ruby glanced around. "I can't see any tracks. Can you tell where Canterlope went next?"

Topaz shook her head. "Maybe my light

will help." Her gemstone glowed and light shined out from Topaz's yellow-brown scales, illuminating the area around them.

"I don't see anything. Do you?" Topaz asked.

"No, but unicorns can jump really high. They make the hoops in their village higher every season," Ruby said. "Maybe Canterlope leaped over this area."

She led Topaz farther into the forest until suddenly Ruby said, "I see something!"

She rushed to a spot on the ground where the dead leaves had been disturbed. Carved into the soil underneath was the unmistakable hoofprint of a unifoal. "There!" Ruby kept searching and found three more. The front edges of the hoofprints were deepest, as if the unifoal had landed, then leaped off again.

"This is him!" Ruby cried. "It must be Canterlope. This way!"

Ruby and Topaz followed the hoofprints. Soon they found more hoofprints, as though Canterlope had come down from another great bound. Then another set, and another. They were heading deeper into the forest, but Ruby was excited to be on the right track.

After a while, the hoofprints got closer and closer together, until finally they were so close, Ruby could tell Canterlope had stopped leaping and had started to walk.

"Oh no! Maybe he was hurt." She gazed through the tree trunks. "Please say Canterlope is okay."

"I hope so," said Topaz, then seeing the

worry on Ruby's face, she added, "We'll find him."

The tracks took them around tree trunks, to the left, then to the right, and back on themselves.

"He was lost," Ruby said, pointing at a place where the hoofprints crossed over each other. "Poor Canterlope. But I can't tell where he went."

She peered into the darkness. Topaz's light shined outward, but didn't illuminate too far.

"Maybe he's close," Topaz said. "It doesn't look like the tracks go much farther."

"We have to find him." Ruby strode to their right. "Canterlope!" she called. "CANTERLOPE!"

Topaz trudged to their left. "Canterlope. Canterlope!"

They kept calling out as they moved slowly around, making sure their voices were carried in every direction.

Finally, Ruby heard a little sound.

"Shush!" she told Topaz. "Do you hear that?"

It was a scraping noise. Ruby gazed up and saw a squirrel scratching at a tree branch. Her shoulders slumped.

"It's a squirrel. I really hoped it was Canterlope. I don't know where else to look!"

The snow was starting to fall faster now, and a clump of snowflakes collected on Ruby's head. She shivered and pushed it to the ground.

"Maybe we should go back to Sparkle Cave," Topaz said in a small voice. "I don't want to give up on Canterlope, but it's only going to get harder to find him in the snow. And we're going to be too cold."

Ruby stared at her friend. "Canterlope's going to be cold too."

Topaz sighed. "I wish Sapphire had been right about Canterlope hiding in a barn. Do you think that, maybe, perhaps, it's possible . . . I mean, could these tracks be old?"

Ruby peered around. "I don't know. Do you think they are? Did I bring us in here for nothing? I'm the worst dragon and the worst friend." She collapsed on the ground.

"No, you're not," Topaz said, but Ruby wasn't listening. She took a closer look

at the hoofprints. There was one set
that pointed toward a large tree trunk.
Maybe . . .

"Wait! Shine your light this way," she
told Topaz. Her friend obeyed, and they
both followed the prints.

They walked around the large tree
and on the other side found a deep
hollow. Topaz got low and shined her light
inside.

Two eyes blinked open. They stared.
They moved, coming closer.

Topaz and Ruby backed up, but then a
young voice shouted, "Ruby! Topaz! You
found me!"

chapter seven

A DARK AND STORMY NIGHT

Canterlope's horn glistened in Topaz's light as he emerged from the hollow in the tree trunk.

He bounced around the two Gemstone Dragons. "You found me! You found me! I was so scared all by myself out here. I'm so happy you found me!"

Ruby hugged Canterlope around his neck and Topaz rubbed his nose.

"I was so worried about you, Canterlope," Ruby said. "Are you all right? I thought you were hurt."

She leaned back to inspect him, making sure the unifoal didn't have any cuts or bruises.

Canterlope showed off each of his sides. "I'm okay. I was really frightened. I couldn't find my way out of the forest, and I thought I'd never get home."

"We'll get you home," Ruby said. "I'm sorry about the fire, Canterlope. I didn't mean to scare you." She looked down at the ground.

"It was an accident," Canterlope said. "I'm sorry I got lost! I should've stayed with Honeydoo, but I panicked. I missed the bridge and ran into a clearing in the trees. I don't know why. I was just trying to get away, but then I couldn't find my way back."

Topaz looked at Ruby. "It's exactly like you said. How did you know?"

"Yeah, how did you find me?" Canterlope beamed up at Ruby.

Ruby shrugged. "I don't know. I guess because I'm young too, I think like you.

When I get scared, I do things but don't always think first. So I imagined what I would've done if I'd been scared off from the fire, and it brought us straight to you."

"Thank you," Canterlope said.

He shivered and Ruby put her arm around his back. "We need to get you home. You must be freezing. I'm cold and I haven't been out here nearly as long as you have."

Canterlope nodded. "Even curled up in the tree was cold. Yes, let's go."

"Oh no." Ruby's eyes widened. "Which way do we go? I was so worried about finding you, I didn't think to mark a trail."

"I didn't either. I think it's this way," Topaz said, shining her light brighter. They headed back the way they had come.

Snow was falling heavily now. It swirled around them, making it difficult for Ruby to see the path. The floor of the forest was becoming coated in white. In the trees, piles of snow were collecting on the branches, then dropping with a loud *THWUMP* onto the ground.

"It's getting harder to see," Topaz said, and Ruby nodded.

Wind had picked up. It whistled around the tree trunks and made the air thick with snow.

"Topaz, your light!" Ruby pointed to where Topaz's light was shining in front of them. "It looks like a wall."

Topaz groaned. "My light is reflecting off the snow and ice in the air. Instead of lighting up the path, it's making it even

harder to see." The topaz gemstone in her chest stopped glowing as the light around her disappeared. "Can you see better without it?"

Ruby peered through the swirls of snow but shook her head. "I can barely see you!"

"The snow is getting thicker," Topaz said, glancing up at the falling flakes.

"The wind is getting stronger," Ruby said, listening to its howls through the forest.

"And everything's getting colder," Canterlope said, shivering more than ever.

"The snowstorm has turned into a blizzard." Topaz looked at Ruby. "I hate to say this, but I don't think we can get home."

"But we have to!" Ruby hugged

Canterlope close. "We have to get him back."

"Look around us, Ruby," Topaz said, gesturing to the snow-blanketed ground. "Can you even see anything? We could get more lost if we try. We could trip over a root or rock buried in the snow and get hurt. We can't take that chance."

Ruby's eyes filled with sadness as she looked at Canterlope. "I'm sorry, Canterlope. Even my rescue isn't good. Topaz is right. We can't get home now."

Canterlope nuzzled Ruby. "That's okay. I have you two with me. This is the best rescue I've ever had."

"How many rescues have you had?" Topaz asked.

Canterlope thought for a bit. "Well, this is my first. But I like it."

Topaz laughed. But Ruby didn't think anything was funny about this. Canterlope had gotten lost because of her, and she couldn't even get him home safely.

chapter eight

COLD, COLD, EVERYWHERE

"What are we going to do now?" Ruby peered through the thick snowfall at the white-covered forest. She had been so worried about finding Canterlope, she hadn't thought about getting back home or how she'd keep him safe. Now they were all stuck, lost in the forest in the middle of a blizzard. Panic rose in Ruby's throat faster than Garnet could fly across the sky.

"We need to find a place to stay the night," Topaz said. She patted Ruby's shoulder as if she could sense her friend's fear.

"We could go back to the tree hollow, but . . ." Canterlope glanced around. "I don't know where it is now. How far have we walked?"

"Too far," Topaz said. "We'll never find it again in this storm. Let's look for somewhere close. Come on, Ruby."

Ruby trudged behind Topaz and Canterlope as they searched for anywhere that they could be safe. A hollow in another tree, perhaps. A small cave. Even a rock big enough to protect their backs.

But all they found was tree trunk after tree trunk, and a ground rapidly filling up with snow.

"We're never going to find a safe enough place!" Ruby wailed. "We might as well just stay here."

Topaz looked around, then nodded. "Actually, that's a good idea, Ruby. We can rest inside this cluster of trees." She pointed at a group of five trunks that had grown up close together. "They'll protect us from some of the wind, at least."

Ruby surveyed the trunks. "I guess we can sit together to keep each other warm."

"Use your fire power, Ruby," Canterlope said. "Then we'll all be super warm!"

But Ruby shook her head. "I can't. I might set the whole of Friendly Forest on fire."

"Ruby—" Topaz began, but Ruby didn't want to hear any more. She walked into the cluster of trees and started sweeping away the snow with her tail. When she'd cleared an area big enough for all three of them, Ruby collapsed into a heap on the wet ground.

Canterlope looked up at Topaz with sad eyes, and Topaz gave him a sad smile back.

"Come on, Canterlope," Topaz said, "let's cuddle."

Topaz and Canterlope huddled next to Ruby, and Ruby's panic finally started to lessen.

She still felt like the worst Gemstone Dragon in the world, though. If she'd only been better at using her power, she would never have started the fire, Canterlope would never have run away, and she

wouldn't have put Topaz in danger by coming out to look for the unifoal.

The howl of the wind racing around the tree trunks was getting louder, and the cracking of twigs as they broke under the heavy snow and ice made Ruby tremble. What if the blizzard never stopped? What if they never found their way home?

"Does anyone want to play a game?" Topaz asked, and Ruby knew she was trying to get Canterlope's mind off the cold.

It must've worked, because Canterlope said excitedly, "I Spy! I'll start." He peered around. "I spy with my unifoal eye something beginning with *S*."

"Squirrel?" asked Topaz.

Canterlope shook his head.

"Snow," said Ruby, gloomily.

"Yes!" Canterlope grinned. "You go now, Topaz."

"Okay." Topaz shivered, then said, "I spy with my dragon eye something beginning with *I.*"

"Insect?" Canterlope asked, but after Topaz shook her head, Ruby answered, "Icicle."

"Yes, that's it," Topaz said, and shivered even more.

Snow was starting to settle on their heads and shoulders. Ruby shook to get it off, but it didn't stop the cold from penetrating their little circle.

Suddenly Ruby heard, "*Tat tat tat tat tat tat.*"

She sat up straight. "What's that noise?"

"I don't know," said Topaz, glancing around.

"Me neither," said Canterlope, his voice rattling.

"*Tat tat tat tat tat.*"

"It's your teeth!" Ruby said. "They're chattering."

"Sorry," Canterlope said. "I'm just so cold."

Topaz stood up quickly, snow dropping off her head. "This is ridiculous! We're Gemstone Dragons. Ruby, you have power over fire! You could warm us all up, but you're being too stubborn."

"I am not being stubborn." Ruby sat up. "You saw what I did before. I can't control my power. I might set this whole forest ablaze. Even in this storm! And I won't be able to stop it." She curled up tighter, crossing her arms over her chest.

"It's okay." Topaz sighed. "I'll find some dry twigs and make us a fire. It won't be as good as yours, but it'll be something."

Watching her friend poke around the ground, Ruby felt terrible. Topaz was a good friend. She hadn't had to come with Ruby to find Canterlope, but she'd come, even though she knew a storm was coming. In fact, Topaz always helped Ruby. She had made Ruby feel better when she couldn't do her tricks. Topaz was trying to help them now, and Ruby knew that she should help as well, but she couldn't. If Ruby was being truly honest with herself, she knew that the fire in the forest hadn't only been caused because she hadn't controlled her power, but because she had let her anger take over.

She'd told herself she would never use her power again, and she had meant it. She couldn't trust herself to not get frustrated or angry and lose control. She couldn't put the forest and her friends in danger again.

Canterlope nosed a stick out of the snow. "Will this do?"

"It's really wet," Topaz said, "but I can try."

She held up the twig and breathed on it. A small ball of fire engulfed the twig, then disappeared. Topaz felt the bark.

"Is it drier?" Canterlope asked.

"Barely," Topaz said. She tried again, this time inhaling deeper to try to make a bigger fire. But all she could breathe out was the small fireball that every dragon could create. Every dragon except Ruby.

"Maybe we could find better sticks if we could see more," Canterlope said to Topaz.

"I'll make some light," Topaz said. "It won't light the way through the storm, but at least it'll help us search right here."

The topaz gemstone in her chest began to glow, and light shined all around her, just enough so they could see into the trees above them.

Ruby watched carefully. Topaz made it look so easy to control her power. She didn't look like she was concentrating the way Diamond had said or standing in any particular way like Amber had suggested.

Topaz looked relaxed and happy, as if she and her power were partners. Not as if she were trying to control it at all.

"There!" Canterlope said, pointing his hoof at a bunch of small twigs that were protected under a bigger branch. "Maybe those are still dry."

"Good thinking, Canterlope," Topaz said. "It's not far. I can fly up and get them."

Topaz stretched her wings just a little. Her yellow-brown scales glistened in the icy air. Then, with a flap, Topaz lifted off.

"Be careful," Ruby called out, as Topaz rose up through the branches to where they'd spied the twigs. The wind was strong and the tree trunks were close together. Ruby was worried about her friend.

Topaz reached out, snapped off the sticks she needed, and started back down. "Easy!" She grinned down at Ruby and Canterlope.

But then a gust of wind shrieked around the trees. It plowed into Topaz and knocked her against a big trunk.

"Topaz!" Ruby and Canterlope shouted together.

Topaz's wings fluttered, but she couldn't catch any more air. Ice had built up on her wings, making them stiff and slippery.

Topaz toppled out of the air and landed with a loud *THUMP* in a snow drift.

chapter nine

RUBY'S BIG IMAGINATION

"No!" Ruby raced over to her friend.

Topaz was covered in snow and shivering uncontrollably. She groaned when she moved.

"Are you hurt?" Ruby searched Topaz's wings for scratches or tears, but she couldn't find any.

"Just a bit bruised, I think." Topaz tried to smile, but instead she winced. She lifted up the twigs she had collected from the branch. They looked wet through now. Still, she tried to breath fire onto them, but her small flames sizzled and went out.

"Sorry, Canterlope," Topaz said. "I can't get it to work."

"That's okay," Canterlope said, nuzzling up to Topaz. "Thank you for trying."

They curled up together again, a shivering heap.

Ruby's shoulders slumped. She should be able to help them, but she was so worried she'd make everything worse. "I'm sorry I can't . . ." she began, but she couldn't bring herself to finish her sentence. She was failing the creatures who loved her the most.

"It's okay," Topaz said, waving Ruby

over. "Come curl up. We'll all be warmer if you join us."

Ruby started to step toward them but stopped. They had curled up together before and it hadn't been enough. They'd been so cold that Topaz had risked her life to try to make a tiny little fire. And the blizzard wasn't getting lighter. If anything, the night was just getting colder.

She had to help.

She had to do something.

She was the only dragon who could.

"You make it look so easy to use your power," Ruby said to Topaz. "How did you get your light to move like you did without it spilling everywhere?"

Topaz glanced at Ruby quizzically. "I just asked it to."

Ruby didn't understand. "You asked it to? Didn't you have to concentrate hard and control it somehow?"

"No. Diamond told me I had to do that when I was learning, but it never worked for me." Topaz gave a small chuckle. "He'd get so frustrated with me. But my power isn't as strong as yours and Diamond's, so maybe that's why."

Ruby thought about this. "I don't know. I concentrated so hard to control my power this morning, and it didn't help. I kept thinking about all the things that could go wrong, and it was a good thing I did, because then everything did go wrong!"

"Your Gemstone Dragon power is a part-t-t-t of you," Topaz said, her teeth chattering as she spoke. "It's like your paw or your tail or your nose. You didn't have to force your tail to clean off the snow on the ground for us. You just did it. You don't have to worry about your power. Trust in it. It'll do what you want-t-t-t-t."

Canterlope lifted his head, his horn shimmering with ice. "I believe in you, Ruby. *Tat-tat-tat-tat-tat.*"

Topaz smiled. "I do too *tat-tat-tat-tat.*"

Ruby frowned. She still wasn't sure she believed in herself, but her friends were freezing. Their teeth were chattering even harder. She wished she could make them warmer.

Suddenly, her gemstone glowed, and a stream of flames shot out from Ruby's mouth. The fire hovered above Topaz and Canterlope, then began to float down toward them. What if it hurt them?

"NO!" Ruby shouted, and she quickly breathed the fire back in.

"That was uni-mazing!" Canterlope said.

"No, it wasn't. The fire was coming right for you." Ruby pouted. "I didn't want it to burn you."

"It wouldn't have burned us," Topaz said. "It was too far away. It looked like it was just going to surround us, to keep us warm."

"It did?" Ruby thought about the fire. "That's what I was imagining it doing."

"And it did!" Topaz said, smiling. "You have such a big imagination, Ruby. But you also imagine the worst things." Topaz tried to laugh, but her teeth were chattering so much, it came out as *"Ta-ta-ta-ta-ta."*

But Ruby didn't laugh. Her eyes widened as a big thought hit her: What if imagining bad things happening was part of the problem? She thought about when she had been trying to juggle and write Canterlope's name. Her power had worked great at first, but as soon as she started imagining all the things that could go wrong, she got worried and couldn't control her power anymore. Maybe she just had to try not to focus on the things that might go wrong. Maybe she had to stay calm so her imagination wouldn't run away from her.

Ruby took a deep breath, trying to push all her nervousness down deep into her belly. *My gemstone power is part of me,* she told herself. *I have to stay calm and focus. I just have to imagine exactly what we need, then trust my fire power to do it.*

Opening her eyes again, Ruby didn't think about her gemstone. She thought about the fire and how she wanted Topaz and Canterlope to be warm. She imagined how wonderful it would be to have a bubble of small flames around the three of them. Enough to keep out the ice and wind and snow. Enough that they wouldn't be cold anymore. But not so much that the flames damaged them or the trees in the forest. A fortress of flame where they could be safe until the morning.

The ruby in her chest glowed and her red scales rippled. She breathed out and

flames danced from her mouth. But this time, they weren't hungry flames, grabbing at the air. The fire gathered in front of Ruby, Topaz, and Canterlope like a friend who was happy to be with them.

Red and orange flickered in Topaz's and Canterlope's eyes, and Ruby got a sudden moment of panic. What if the flames got bigger? What if they got out of control?

Responding to her, the fire started to bite at the air around it. Not friendly anymore. Like it was angry.

Ruby's eyes widened. This was exactly what she had been afraid of!

But instead of Diamond's voice, this time Topaz's words echoed in Ruby's mind. "Trust yourself. Imagine good things."

Ruby took a deep breath, and as she

calmed herself, so did the flames. Ruby smiled. Her fire power was working! In response to Ruby's excitement, the fire did a little bounce in the air.

"Go . . ." Ruby whispered. She blew lightly on her flames, imagining what she wanted them to do.

The fire spread out into a giant bubble, encasing Topaz, Canterlope, and Ruby inside. It wasn't too close to any tree trunks, so Ruby felt good that it wouldn't damage the forest.

Wind howled around them. Snow and ice dropped from the trees and sky above. But anything that touched the fire fortress just melted away.

"This is uni-rific." Canterlope scampered around the small space inside the fortress. "My teeth aren't even chattering anymore!"

"It's perfect, Ruby." Topaz smiled at her friend. "You've saved us. I knew you could."

Ruby smiled back. She hadn't believed in herself, but with the help of those who loved her, she had used her power well.

chapter ten

HOME SWEET HOMECOMING

* * * * * *

The next morning, Ruby woke up to Canterlope shouting.

"Oh no!" Ruby jumped up. "What happened? Are you hurt?"

Canterlope pointed his horn to the treetops. "Look at the blue sky! The blizzard is gone."

Topaz yawned. "That was the best night's sleep I've had in a while. I think you should make me a fire fortress every night, Ruby."

Ruby laughed as she let the fire fortress die out. "You helped me, so I guess I owe you."

Canterlope pranced around, jumping into snow drifts and then back out again. "The fields are probably covered with good snow at home. Oooh, we can slide down Mineral Mountain!"

"We have to get out of the forest first," Ruby said, glancing around her. "Every direction looks the same. I still can't tell where we should go."

Topaz slumped. "The snow has covered all our tracks from last night."

Just then, a strange noise came from overhead.

"What is that?" Ruby asked. "I've never heard a bird make a sound like that."

Topaz shrugged. "Me neither."

Canterlope smiled. "That's not a bird. Look!"

He pointed to the sky with his horn. Ruby and Topaz gazed up in time to see a streak of pink cross above the treetops. Behind it came the words, "Ruuuubyyyyy. Tooopaaaaaazzzz. Caaannnteeeeerrrrrllll-llooooope."

"It's Garnet!" Ruby shouted. "We're here! We're down here!" She jumped up and down waving her arms. But Garnet had already flown off.

"See?" Ruby said. "I told you he can't see anything down here when he's flying so fast."

Topaz laughed. "At least we can follow his direction. He probably came from Sparkle Cave, so let's go that way."

Ruby and Topaz told jokes as Canterlope leaped around them all the way to the edge of the Friendly Forest. When they finally got to the Crystal River, they found a crowd of unicorns, goblins, gnomes, and dragons. None of them looked up at Ruby, Topaz, and Canterlope. They were all too busy worrying.

"What's wrong?" Ruby asked the nearest unicorn. "Has something happened?"

The unicorn hung his head. "Oh, it's the saddest thing. We still can't find young Canterlope."

Canterlope's ears pricked up. "I'm right here!"

The eyes of all the creatures turned their way. The unicorns' horns glowed brightly with happiness.

"Canterlope!" Honeydoo jumped over to them. "You're all right!"

"Of course I am!" Canterlope said. "Topaz and Ruby found me. They kept me safe and warm all night."

He beamed at Ruby and Topaz, and Ruby's heart felt like it would burst, she was so happy.

Sapphire strolled up to Ruby. "I see I was right about you."

Ruby lowered her gaze. "Oh Sapphire, I know you told us to stay in Sparkle Cave, but I found these hoofprints. Don't blame Topaz. I just couldn't let—"

"I meant," Sapphire said, "that you are a

very smart and brave Gemstone Dragon. And you knew exactly what had to be done."

Ruby lifted her eyes to meet Sapphire's. The deep blue dragon smiled down at Ruby, warming her heart.

All of Gemstone Valley decided the rescue deserved a celebration. So that evening, they gathered in Shimmering Hall for a feast.

As the last rays of sun drifted through the giant magical Gemstone Dragon image embedded in the far wall of the cave, platters of food were piled high onto the tabletops.

The menu included all the favorite foods of Canterlope, Topaz, and Ruby. There were haybale pumpkin balls and grass-stuffed apple strudel for Canterlope; zucchini zinc boats and lemon-silicon shortbread for Topaz; and carrot-sulfur tacos and blueberry-chromium cake for Ruby.

Obsidian, Opal, and the goblins had outdone themselves in the Sparkle Cave kitchen. Ruby couldn't believe how good all the dishes were—even Canterlope's

grass-stuffed apple strudel, which had sounded very unappealing. Once she tasted it, Ruby had to have a second helping.

By the end of the meal, every Gemstone Valley resident was stuffed full and ready for bed. Everyone ambled outside of Sparkle Cave. Unlike the blustery night before, the sky was full of stars and the light from a bright moon made the snow on the ground glisten. One wayward star swept across the night, and Ruby oohed along with Topaz.

Canterlope and Honeydoo ambled up to Ruby and Topaz. Canterlope had a shy smile on his face.

"Ruby? Topaz? Thank you again for bringing me home." His hoof dug into the snow on the ground. "I know it must've been hard for you to come after me, but you saved me."

"Yes," piped up Honeydoo, her horn glimmering in the moonlight. "Thank you for rescuing my friend."

They both nuzzled Ruby and Topaz, who beamed.

"Let's hope you don't need to be rescued a second time. I'm not sure we could top this one," Topaz said, and everyone laughed.

"Come on, Canterlope and Honeydoo," called Canterlope's mother. "It's past your bedtime."

Canterlope and Honeydoo started to follow the others down to Gemstone Valley, but then Canterlope stopped and galloped back.

"Ruby, could you do one more thing for me?" he asked.

"Anything!" she said.

"Could you finish spelling my name in the fire?" Canterlope gazed up at her hopefully. Honeydoo ambled back. "Yes! Yes! Please do."

Panic started to grow in Ruby's belly again, and she wished she hadn't said she'd do anything. She was proud of the fire fortress she'd made in the forest, but what if she couldn't use her power like that again? All the Gemstone Dragons and Gemstone Valley creatures were watching. What if she messed up?

Topaz squeezed Ruby's paw as though she could tell what Ruby was thinking.

"She'd love to," Topaz said to Canterlope. Then she turned to Ruby. "Show us what your big imagination can do."

Focus on the good in my imagination, Ruby thought. *Yes, that's what I have to do.*

Ruby smiled and said, "I'd love to."

As her ruby gemstone glowed, she imagined *CANTERLOPE* in flaming letters up in the sky. And not only the name; she imagined the letters dancing around like prancing unicorns. She gently breathed out a fireball, and the flames jumped and twisted in the air.

"*C!*" Canterlope and Honeydoo shouted, as the letter came into view. Then, "*A! . . . N! . . . T! . . .*"

Before long, the night sky was lit up

with *CANTERLOPE* galloping above them. All the Gemstone Dragons and their friends applauded and cheered. Ruby felt like she could soar, but her fiery trick needed something else—someone else.

"Topaz," Ruby called, "what about Honeydoo?"

Topaz grinned. "Great idea!" The gemstone in her chest glowed as light spun into the sky and spelled out *HONEYDOO*.

Honeydoo and Canterlope pranced under their names. Other unifoals asked for their names in the sky, and other Gemstone Dragons happily obeyed. Soon the sky was full of names made up from different gemstone powers. It was the most beautiful sight Ruby had ever seen.

"Thank you, Ruby. You do the best tricks," Canterlope said before he and Honeydoo raced off to Gemstone Valley with the other creatures.

"He's absolutely right," Topaz said, as she walked with Ruby back into Sparkle Cave and to their bedcaves.

"I don't know," Ruby said.

Topaz frowned and stopped her friend. "Oh, Ruby, do you still think you can't control your power, after all that?"

"No, no," Ruby said. "I do, but I've just had an idea for some new tricks that are even better! I'll need to practice, though. I want to get them just right. Can you help me build a new bonfire tomorrow? It'll have to be even bigger. It's not going to snow tomorrow, is it? This will be the best trick, and . . . oh! I just had an idea for another one!"

Topaz laughed. "I think you're going to do just fine."

Ruby smiled. "Me too."

SOME FACTS ABOUT RUBIES!

COLOR: Rubies are red. They get their color from a mineral called chromium. Some rubies have tints of orange, pink, or purple.

BIRTHSTONE: Ruby is the birthstone of people born in July.

MEANING: Rubies were once believed to protect warriors in battle. They are also associated with love, power, and energy.

FUN FACTS: Rubies are among the rarest gemstones. They are one of only four gems that are considered precious, along with emeralds, sapphires, and diamonds.

JOIN THE
GEMSTONE DRAGONS
IN ANOTHER EXCITING
ADVENTURE!

Turn the page for a sneak peek . . .

Opal stretched up onto her toes, holding two picture frames as high on the cave wall as she could.

"Here?" She peered over her shoulder at her friend, but Aquamarine was frowning.

"It's difficult to see what it'll look like with you standing there." Aquamarine twitched his wings.

"That's no problem." Opal concentrated

on the opal gemstone on her chest and felt its power flow through her body. Her rainbow scales rippled as she turned invisible. Now the picture frames were all that could be seen hanging from the cave wall. "What do you think now?"

Aquamarine scrunched up his nose. "I don't know if I want them both there."

"You'd better hurry up and decide or we'll be late for dinner," Opal said.

Aquamarine waved his paw. "We've got plenty of time. I promise we won't be late."

"I hope not. Tonight Sapphire's going to announce which Gemstone Dragon will give the Friendship Festival speech. I wonder who it'll be." Opal gasped. "Maybe it'll be you, Aquamarine!"

"Me? Nah. I gave it a while ago." He

walked to the other side of his cave to view his decorations from a different angle. "I think it should be you. You've never given the Friendship Festival speech. You'd be great!"

Opal toppled off her toes. "Me? You're funny." She laughed, then stretched to hold the frames up again. "I hope it's Topaz. I loved the speech she gave last year. It was so inspiring!"

"All she did was talk about the sun, and how we need to be the light. We don't need light. We need brilliance!" Aquamarine raised his arms as if to demonstrate how brilliant his cave would be . . . if only he could decide where to put the pictures. He dropped his arms again. "Try making one disappear."

Opal chuckled, then concentrated on her opal gemstone. The picture frame in her left paw disappeared. "How's this?"

Aquamarine flopped down on his bed. "I don't know. Something's not right but I can't put my claw on it. Give me the disappeared frame. Maybe it'll look better with each picture on a different side."

Opal handed the frame to him, but it went right through his outstretched paw. "Sorry, I keep forgetting that when I make something invisible it can go through things. Hold on," she said.

Opal made herself and the frame visible again, then handed it over. Aquamarine placed it against the wall over his bedrock, but shook his head. "That's not it."

Opal glanced at the frame she still had

in her paw. She had never been good at making decisions either. That's why she decorated her bedcave with flowers and changed them every week.

"I don't know, Aquamarine," she said, placing the frame on his rock desk. "But you need to decide quickly. Everyone from Gemstone Valley is going to be at dinner for the announcement, and Shimmering Hall will be packed! I want to get a good seat."

SAMANTHA M. CLARK is a storyteller, a daydreamer, and the author of a number of books for young readers. Most of the time, she lives in her head with a magical tree, a forest of talking animals, and a sky filled with pink fluffy clouds. Like the Gemstone Dragons, she knows the best power in the world is friendship.

JANELLE ANDERSON is an illustrator who is happiest when bringing the images in her head to life. Some of her favorite things to draw are colorful mountains, sparkly waterfalls, and magical creatures just like the Gemstone Dragons. She loves the outdoors and making people smile, and believes there is a little bit of magic in everyone.